The Berenstain Bears

CLEAN HOUSE

D1021580

By Stan & Jan Berenstain

HarperCollins*Publishers*

"It is spring," said Mama Bear.

"It is time to clean our house."

"I will help," said Papa.

"I will help," said Brother.

"I will help," said Sister.

"Good," said Mama.

"We will clean our house

from the top to the bottom,

from the bottom to the top."

4

They started at the bottom.

"My goodness," said Mama.

"There are too many things.

It is hard to clean with so many things."

"We will have a yard sale," said Papa.

"We will put some in the yard."

"This old fish," said Brother.

"It is dusty."

"This stuffed owl," said Sister.

"It is musty."

"This old fishing pole,"

said Mama.

"It is bent."

"Those are my things,"

said Papa.

"But it is spring.

We must clean house.

I will put them in the yard."

They went upstairs
to the living room.

10

"There are too many things," said Papa.

"We must put some in the yard," said Mama.

"This old lamp," said Brother.

"It has a crack."

"This old pillow," said Sister.

"It has a spot on the back."

12

"This old stool," said Papa.

"It has a tear."

"Those are my things,"
said Mama.
"But I will put them
in the yard."

Then they went upstairs.

Brother and Sister's room

had many, many things.

"My goodness!" said Mama.

"There are too many things in this room.

We must put some in the yard."

"This baseball bat," said Papa.

"It is split."

"This teddy bear," said Mama.

"The stuffing is coming out of it."

"These old games and toys," said Papa. "They would be fun for other girls and boys."

"Those are our things," said Brother and Sister. "We will put them in the yard."

"Yes, it is spring," said Mama.

"We must clean our house

from the top to the bottom,

from the bottom to the top."

But there was something they forgot!

They forgot the attic!

"My goodness!" said Mama.

"We forgot the attic."

They went up to the attic.

It was bad.

"My goodness!" said Mama.

"There are too many things!"

"Yes," said Papa.

"Many too many

to put in the yard."

They went downstairs.

They went out to
the yard.

They made a sign.

It said YARD SALE TODAY.

23

They looked at the things
they put in the yard.

"This is hard," said Papa.
"I love those things
I put in the yard."

24

"This is hard," said Mama.

"I love those things

I put in the yard."

"This is hard,"

said Brother and Sister.

"We love those things

we put in the yard."

They took them up
to the attic.

They put them with the other

old things they loved.

"We have done our job," said Mama.

"But we are not done," said Brother.

"We have not cleaned the attic," said Sister.

"We are done," said Mama.

"But the attic will not go away.

We will clean the attic

another day."